We hope you enjoy this boo
Please return or renew it by
You can renew it at **www.no**
or by using our free library ap   you can
phone **0344 800 8020** - please have your library
card and pin ready.
You can sign up for email reminders too.

NORFOLK COUNTY COUNCIL
LIBRARY AND INFORMATION SERVICE

First published in 2010 in Great Britain by
Barrington Stoke Ltd
18 Walker Street, Edinburgh, EH3 7LP

www.barringtonstoke.co.uk

ISBN: 978-1-84299-767-3

Printed in Great Britain by Bell & Bain Ltd

Check out the 5 Lords of Pain website:

www.fivelordsofpain.co.uk

For amazing downloads, behind-the-scenes action and exclusive extracts from the next books ...

The 5 Lords of Pain Books

1. The Lord of the Mountain

2. The Lord of the Void

3. The Lord of Tears

4. The Lord of the Typhoon

5. The Lord of Fire

Contents

	The Story So Far	1
1	The Face at the Window	3
2	At the Dojo	13
3	Green Tea and Honour	23
4	The Legend	29
5	A Hero No One Had Ever Heard Of	45
6	Time for a New TV	59
7	Jimmy Blue	66
8	Hail Storm	76
9	The Lord of the Void	80
10	Shwoop	87
11	Black Swords	96
12	The Black Element Gem	107
13	Sharif	109
	List of Japanese Words	114
	Sneak peek at the next book!	118

The Story So Far

The Contest takes place every 30 years. It's a series of duels between five demons and a single human champion. What is at stake is no less than the future of the whole world.

The human champion is always a member of the Yamada family. The task of defeating the demons, who are known as the Five Lords of Pain, is passed down from father to son. It has been that way for many hundreds of years.

Tom Yamada is the latest in line to face the Five Lords. Tom is only fifteen, and his Contest isn't due to start until he is 30. But something has gone wrong. Now Tom finds himself having to fight the duels long before he is supposed to.

Dragon is Tom's trainer. He teaches him the one-to-one skills he needs for the duels. These skills are called the martial arts. Dragon knew his young pupil was not ready for the first duel. Jane Yamada, Tom's mother, thought the same.

But Tom showed them they were wrong by winning the first duel. He beat the first demon, a monster who looked and fought like a Sumo wrestler. This was the Lord of the Mountain.

Two months have passed. Now Tom is getting ready for the next duel ...

Chapter 1

The Face at the Window

There was a scream.

Tom ran to the bathroom.

His mother was standing at the basin, in her bathrobe. She was about to have a shower, and had been taking out her contact lenses.

Now she was staring at the bathroom window. Her whole body was stiff. Her eyes stood out.

"What is it?" Tom asked.

"I – I'm not sure," said his mother, her voice shaking. "I thought I saw something. Something out there."

She pointed to the window.

"It was ... a face," she said. "A face, right there. Up close to the glass. Looking in. Looking in at me."

Tom felt the hairs on the back of his neck prickle.

There couldn't have been a face at the window. *Couldn't* have been.

Because he and his mother lived on the third floor.

"No, you're wrong, Mum," he said. "You're being silly. It must have been something else."

"It was a face," his mother insisted. "It was wrapped in this kind of white cloth, a bit like a turban. The cloth covered its nose and mouth, but I could see some of its skin. The skin was pale. And the eyes ..."

She shuddered.

"The eyes were quite white," she said, almost in a whisper. "Like the eyes of a dead fish. And they were staring right at me!"

"OK, now you're really freaking me out, Mum," Tom said.

"Well, excuse me," said his mother. "I just had the wits scared out of me, but oh, no, we mustn't freak *you* out, must we, Tom?"

Taking no notice of the sting in her voice, Tom went to the window. It was small, no more than 50 centimetres square. The face would almost have filled it – if there had been a face at all.

The back of the house looked out onto a large park. Tom could see nothing out there but trees. Their branches swayed in the darkness.

He opened the window with a shaking hand. He was shaking even more when he poked his head out.

The moon was full and bright, giving plenty of light to see by. London, anyway, was never truly dark at night. The sky above the city was lit up by all the street lamps and house lights.

Tom peered up, down, to the right, to the left. Above, all he could see was the next floor up, and the gutter that ran along the line of the roof. Right below him there was the rear garden, with its lawn, pond and decking. On both sides there were houses, just the same as his, tall and sturdy Victorian buildings. That was all. He couldn't see a person anywhere.

Could somebody have climbed up to the window?

No. It wasn't possible. The back of the house was a sheer brick wall, with very few gaps that you could slot your hands and feet in. A drain-pipe ran down it, but you would have to be a monkey to get up that, and a small monkey at that. The drain-pipe was made of plastic and so were the clips that fixed it to the wall. It would have broken if a human had tried to climb up that way.

Less than half a minute had passed from the time Tom's mother screamed to the time he opened the window. There was no way someone could have got back down to the ground in half a minute. Not unless they'd just let go and dropped. And then they would be lying in the garden with at least one leg broken, more likely both.

"Well?" said Tom's mother. "Do you see him?"

"Yes, he's floating out there, with a big rocket pack on his back."

"None of your lip, Tom! There *was* a face. I swear it."

Tom turned round. "Mum, do you have your contacts in right now?"

"No."

"So you didn't have them in when you saw the face?"

"No, I'd just popped them out."

"So how can you be sure that what you saw even was a face?"

"I don't see that badly," his mother said. "Things are a bit hazy without my lenses. But even so, a face is a face."

"You didn't perhaps catch sight of the moon," said Tom, "and mistake it for a face?"

"No."

"You don't sound one hundred per cent sure."

"Well, now that you've said it ..." His mother frowned. "I suppose it just might have been the moon. I only saw it for a moment before it vanished in a flash. I was bending down like this." She bent over the basin in the bathroom. "And I spotted something out of the corner of my eye. So I turned my head, and ..."

She gave a thin smile.

"And look," she said, eyeing the window. "There it is. I can see it from this angle. The moon."

She stood up tall, puffing out her cheeks. So it was alright.

"God," she said. "What a twit I am. Of course it was the moon."

"Case solved, madam," said Tom, like a detective on a TV show. "A simple matter of getting the wrong man."

"What an idiot I am," said his mother. "Damn it, I'm just so twitchy these days. Jumping at shadows the whole time. The Contest – it's got me so worried. The black

Element Gem has started fading out. So there's not long left till the Lord of the Void will throw out his challenge to you. I keep thinking about that. I can't get it out of my head."

"Relax, Mum," Tom said. "It's going to be all right. I beat the Lord of the Mountain, didn't I? Without much sweat. And it'll be the same with the other four Lords of Pain, trust me."

Tom sounded confident, but he wasn't really, not deep down. His victory over the Lord of the Mountain hadn't been as easy as he liked to make out.

Still, he *had* won the fight. There was no question about that. And since he'd won one of his five duels, that gave him good reason to think he could win the rest.

"If you say so," said his mother. "Now, close the window, would you? There's a cold wind blowing in."

Tom leaned out to pull the window shut. As he did so, he spotted something.

It was a set of marks on the window-sill outside. Four tiny holes in a row, close together. As if someone had dug something into the sill – a tool, maybe a large fork of some kind.

Tom touched the marks. He pulled off a few chips of painted wood from around them. The chips were sharp and fresh. The wood beneath was new and bright, not dull with age or stained with rain.

These marks weren't old. They were brand new.

"Tom? What is it?"

"Nothing, Mum."

"Well, then, close the window. The wind's going right up my bathrobe."

Tom shut the window.

"Have a nice shower," he said, as he left the room.

Chapter 2
At the Dojo

"A face, eh?" said Dragon, the next morning.

"Yeah," said Tom. "And I really thought Mum must have been seeing things. She's pretty stressed out at the moment. Even more stressed out than she normally is. So I thought she'd spooked herself somehow, that was all. She'd seen the moon and thought it was this pale face with a white cloth wrapped round it. Only now, of course ..."

"Now you're not so sure."

"It was those marks just below the window-sill," Tom said. "They reminded me of something."

"What would that be?" said Dragon. Before Tom could reply, he added, "Oh, by the way – *hai*!"

This was an attack cry. Tom and Dragon were sparring with each other and talking at the same time. Dragon was armed with a *naginata*, a long wooden pole with a curved blade at one end. Tom was defending himself with a *chigiriki*. It was a short stick with a two-foot-long chain attached to it. There was a metal weight at the end of the chain, in the shape of a cylinder with spikes on.

Dragon slashed at Tom with the *naginata*. Its blade flashed. Tom dodged the blow, twirling the *chigiriki*. He tried to wrap the chain around the *naginata* and yank the weapon out of Dragon's hands. But Dragon was too fast for him. He sprang backwards. The *chigiriki* missed the *naginata* by inches.

Tom swung the *chigiriki* back. He caught the chain with his spare hand, just above the metal weight. He planted his feet on the floor and bent his knees, bracing himself for Dragon's next attack.

"What did the marks remind you of?" Dragon asked again. He was gripping the pole of the *naginata* harder.

"*Shuko*," said Tom. "Ninja cat claws. Like the ones over there."

He nodded towards a rack of weapons on the far wall. Among them was a pair of *shuko*. They looked like fingerless gloves with hooks on them. Ninjas were Japanese assassins, masters of stealth and trickery. They would use *shuko* on their hands, just as they would use a set of the same kinds of hooks on the soles of their feet. The two sets of hooks

15

allowed them to scramble up sheer walls pretty much like Spider-Man.

"You believe a ninja scaled the side of your house last night?" said Dragon.

"I don't know," said Tom. "All I know is that if someone did, it could only have been a ninja. And only a ninja could have made a quick getaway like that."

Dragon raised an eye-brow. "Let's suppose the face at the window did belong to a ninja. Why was he there? To spy on your mother in the bathroom?"

"Well, yeah, that's the question, isn't it?" said Tom. "Why? Maybe he was a pervy ninja. A peeping-tom ninja. Gets his kicks watching ladies take showers. When he's not busy bumping people off, I mean."

"Seems a bit odd to me."

"Me too," Tom agreed. "I'm not saying I'm right. Anything could have left those marks on the window ledge. A very big bird, perhaps."

Even Tom had to admit this didn't sound likely.

"But," he went on, "what with everything else that's going on right now, the Contest and all that ... Well, you have to wonder, don't you?"

"Indeed you do," said Dragon. "*Hai!*"

He charged, twirling the *naginata* above him. The blade flashed down at Tom's head. Tom bent to the side just in time, and the *naginata* whisked past his arm. Had he been a split second slower, Dragon would have carved his head in two.

In response, Tom flung the *chigiriki* chain out sideways. But he was off-balance, and his aim was off. The metal weight struck the blade of the *naginata* with a clang, then bounced away.

Dragon was out of range in an instant. He sprang to a corner of the room. He stood there with the *naginata* held at an angle in front of him.

They had been sparring for nearly half an hour. Tom was damp with sweat and worn out, whereas Dragon wasn't even breathing hard. He looked as fresh as when they had started.

Dragon was so fit, it was scary. Sometimes Tom had to wonder if the guy was even human. He was an old man. He must be at least 50, maybe even older. Yet he could still run rings around Tom.

"If it was a ninja," Dragon said, "that would explain the cloth your mother saw. How did she describe it? Wound round his head like a turban?"

"Yes. It was over most of the face."

"A ninja's scarf," said Dragon. "Wrapped around his face to form a hood and mask."

"That was what I was thinking," said Tom. He was swinging the *chigiriki* by his side. "But what about the eyes? She said they were quite white. Like the eyes of a dead fish."

"Hmm," said Dragon.

The two of them began to circle round each other, like tigers waiting to pounce.

"It does remind me of ..." Dragon said. "But no. I always thought that was just a story."

"What was just a story?" Tom asked.

"I don't think it can be true. In fact, it can't be."

"What can't be true?" Tom pressed him. "Come on, clue me in."

"Not now," said Dragon. "Later. I'll need to do some asking around first. Speak to a few friends of mine. It may all be nothing. I could just be jumping at shadows too, same as your mother."

He grinned. His orange-brown eyes twinkled.

"And don't think I haven't noticed what you're up to, Tom."

"What?" Tom said, pretending there was nothing wrong.

"Moving in on me like that. Creeping up. Trying to get within range. You think, because I'm talking, I'm not thinking about the fight."

"Well, are you?"

"I'm –"

"*Hai!*" yelled Tom, as he leapt forward and lashed out with the *chigiriki*. The chain wound itself around the pole of Dragon's *naginata*, three times. Tom gave a great tug, and the naginata flew out of Dragon's hands.

Tom caught it.

"There," he said. "You're disarmed, Dragon. Time to surrender."

With a snap of his wrist, Tom loosed the chain from the *naginata*.

But in the second it took him to do this, Dragon produced another weapon. He shook his arm, and a *tanto* dagger slid out from the sleeve of his *gi* jacket, into his hand.

Next thing Tom knew, the dagger was at his throat.

"You were too confident," Dragon growled. His face was so close to Tom's that Tom could see the flecks of gold in his eyes. "Never think that an enemy is unarmed, just because he does not *seem* to have a weapon. That could be a fatal mistake."

The sharp edge of the *tanto* dagger felt cold against Tom's neck, like a sliver of ice. Tom's moment of success was now a moment of disaster.

"Yes, *sensei*," he said to Dragon, ashamed.

"Good," said Dragon. He lowered the dagger and stepped back. "Then you've learned an important lesson today. Let's break for some tea."

Chapter 3
Green Tea and Honour

"You're not bad at this stuff, *sensei*," Tom said. "Martial arts and that."

"Thank you, Tom," Dragon said with a wry smile. "I'm glad you've noticed. I'd hate to think you were getting your training from a complete no-hoper."

They were sitting cross-legged on either side of a low table. Between them stood a flask made of fine china and full of green tea. They were drinking from small fine china bowls with pictures of cherry blossom on the side. The tea was very hot, and tasted both sweet and bitter.

"But I mean," Tom said, "this is just a wild idea, but why don't *you* face the Lords of Pain instead of me? Come on, it makes sense. You're the great, wise *kung fu* master. I'm just the new boy. You could beat them with one hand tied behind your back."

"Perhaps so," said Dragon. "But I am not a Yamada."

"Yeah, but you could pretend to be me, couldn't you? Just walk up to each Lord of Pain and say, 'Hi, I'm Tom Yamada, pleased to meet you.' Then hit him with the big smackdown before he has a chance to say, 'No, you're not.'"

Dragon grinned. The golden flecks in his eyes danced. "You know that cannot be. For one thing, as I told you at Stonehenge, only a Yamada may pass through the barrier into the demons' world. No other living creature can. For you, it's like walking through a thin layer of mist. If I tried, it would be like walking into a brick wall."

"I know," Tom admitted. "I'm just trying to work out ways of making sure the right side wins the Contest. Saving the world isn't really something you want to mess up, is it?"

"Not really," said Dragon.

"So, what about guns, then?" Tom said. "Why is it that I have to use only martial arts weapons? Couldn't I go in there with an AK-47 and just blow the bad guys away? Better yet, a missile launcher. One squeeze of the trigger, and there'd be chunks of Lord of Pain all over the place."

"I've warned you about playing those video games," said Dragon. "They fill your head with all sorts of strange nonsense. Anyway, guns aren't allowed. The rules of the Contest forbid them."

"Do they? The rules were laid down ages ago, before guns were invented. Does it really say anywhere that I can't use a gun? Why do I have to do this as it's always been done? Why can't I bring things up to date? What's to stop me?"

Dragon took a sip of his tea. He always slurped it round his mouth, in order to give it more flavour.

"History," he said. "It's the custom. Then there's honour. Above all, honour."

"Honour?" said Tom with a laugh. "The Lords of Pain are demons. I don't know much about demons, but I do know that honour isn't something they're famous for. It's not the first thing that springs to mind when you think of demons. Trickery? Cheating? Nastiness? Yes. But not honour."

"Which makes it all the more important that *you* have it, Tom," said Dragon. "Honour is the one thing the Lords of Pain lack. It is the one thing that truly makes you better than them. The Yamadas have honour. They have done what they have to, over the centuries. Without complaint. Without protest. With dignity and courage. Their spirit has been great, while the Lords of Pain are, when all is said and done, nothing but a bunch of greedy bullies. Honour is an idea they cannot understand. They do not prize it. They fight for themselves, for their own selfish ends."

Dragon leaned forward.

"You, Tom," he went on, "fight for the whole world. Fight for billions of people you have never met and will never meet. And that, I believe, is why the Lords of Pain have always lost in the past, and why they will always lose. Honour is your greatest strength, Tom. Better than your hands and feet, better than any sword or knife, better even than a gun. Lose your honour, and you might as well give up."

27

"Yeah," said Tom. "Point taken. All I'm saying is, it's not very fair. The Lords of Pain choose when and where we fight. There's five of them and only one of me. They have magical demon powers and I don't. And I can't even things up? In any way?"

"You know the story, the old legend," said Dragon. This wasn't a question. "You know how and why the Contest began."

"Of course."

"Then you understand why things must be the way they are. They cannot be any other way."

Dragon set down his tea cup.

"And now we must return to your training," he said. "Honour is all well and fine. But it means nothing unless it is backed up by fighting skills."

Chapter 4
The Legend

Tom decided to walk home from the *dojo* instead of taking the bus. It was a warm evening, the first warm evening of the year. Spring had come, waking the world from its winter sleep. Fresh green specks of the new leaves were peeping out on London's trees.

He thought about the legend of the Contest as he walked. It was a story handed down from father to son in the Yamada family. His mother had told it to him time and time again when he was little. Often she had said, "Tonight, Tom, I'm not reading you a bedtime story. Tonight, it's the legend." And she would repeat the legend just as Tom's father had told it to her. She said it was important for Tom to know how the Contest had begun.

But Tom knew that the legend itself was important to his mother. It connected her to her dead husband. It was one way for her to remember him.

The legend went like this.

Once, long ago, in an age before history, demons walked the earth.

They lived alongside humans, in the cities and in the country. They kept away from people for the most part. They stuck with their own kind and did not often deal with men. But still they were there.

It wasn't rare to see a demon strolling along a road, or sitting in a tree, brooding about life, or perhaps sailing across the sky on bat-like wings. The demons had their own laws and customs, and you couldn't really say they were friendly. But they weren't enemies either. No one quite trusted them. But no one was scared of them. The demons were a part of normal life. People treated them the way hunters treated snakes or bears. Not a danger so long as you left them alone.

But five of the demons *were* dangerous.

They were arch-demons, members of the ruling class in the demon world. They were powerful and proud, and they had more magic than any others of their kind. Each had been born with an Element Gem in his heart. The gems contained the force of the five elements from which everything in the universe was formed. One was earth, one was water, one was wind, one was fire, and one was the void, which was just empty space with nothing in it, such as you find between the planets and the stars.

These five arch-demons looked around them and did not like what they saw. They didn't understand why their fellow demons chose to live the way they did, sharing the earth with the humans, when they really should be ruling it. After all, the demon race was better than the human race in every way.

Demons lived for hundreds of years, sometimes even for thousands of years. Humans only lasted till 70 or so, and that was if they were lucky.

Demons had strong bodies. They did not get sick like humans did. Their bones did not break as easily. Even the weakest of them was far stronger and fitter than an ordinary person.

Above all, demons could work magic. A human could become a wizard or a witch only after years of learning and practice, and, even then, humans could never be really skilled in the magical arts. In most cases magic either destroyed them or sent them mad. But, for a demon, magic came as easily as breathing.

In other words, humans were not on the same level as demons. They were lesser beings, and should be taught their place.

Or so the five arch-demons felt. They couldn't see why humans shouldn't be slaves of the demon race.

And so they began to plot to take over the earth and run it the way they wanted. They decided to call themselves the Five Lords of Pain, and their plan was to bring all the world's demons together, train them into one army, and attack. They would kill half the human race. The humans who were left would spend their lives working for the demons. They would grow food for them, wait on them as servants, clean up after them, fetch water, dig, scrub – all the hard and filthy jobs. Their children would do the same, and their

children's children, and so on for ever and
ever.

The Five Lords of Pain spoke in secret to all
their fellow demons. They stirred them up
against humans. They made every demon in
the world frantic with fury. They promised
them a wonderful future, when demons would
be the masters and humans would be like
cattle.

Then, when the moment was right and the
demons were at their most angry, they began
their attack. Thousands of them swarmed
across the earth. They burned whole towns to
the ground. They killed men, women and
children. They burned down crops. They cut
down forests. They tore down temples. They
stole everything from palaces. Everywhere
they went, they took death and destruction
with them.

People fought back, here and there, but
they were no match for such an enemy. There

were ten humans to every demon, but the demons were twenty times more powerful. It was a war the human race could not hope to win.

Then, just when it seemed that all was lost, a hero appeared.

He was a Japanese warrior and his name was Yoshiro Yamada. He was famous in his homeland, and known as the greatest living samurai. He was well trained in all the martial arts. No one could get the better of him in combat. No one even dared to try any more. Yoshiro Yamada was too fast with his sword. Everyone knew that to fight him was to die.

The last man Yamada had killed had been a bandit. The bandit had had no idea who Yamada was. Otherwise he would not have stopped him on the road one night and held up a knife and told him to hand over all his money.

Yoshiro Yamada took one look at the man and said, "Do you know that I am a samurai? That I am a senior warrior, that my job is to guard the Emperor himself?"

The bandit laughed. "I see that you are armed," he said. "I see also that I am holding a knife to your neck, while your sword is still by your side."

Yamada nodded. "It does seem as if you may have won this fight. But tell me. Do you blink?"

The bandit frowned. "Of course I blink. Everyone blinks."

"I am able to draw my sword and run it through you in the time it takes you to blink," said Yamada. "Do you believe that?"

"Of course not!" snorted the bandit. "No man can do that. No man is that quick."

"Then blink, and I'll prove it," said Yamada.

The bandit stared at him.

Then, making a big show of it, the bandit blinked.

He looked down, and found Yamada's sword sunk in his chest, up to the hilt.

"I believe you now," he said with a gasp, and fell to the ground, dead.

That had been many years ago. Yoshiro Yamada had not had to kill anyone since then. He was no longer working for the Emperor and was living a peaceful life on his farm just outside Tokyo, with his wife, son, and plenty of chickens.

But he could no longer stay at home when the demons started ravaging the earth. He chased the demons across Japan, slaying them by the dozen. Most other people were afraid and hid from the demons. But Yamada went looking for the creatures and killed them wherever he found them.

But more of the demons came, and still more. Yamada worked hard, but he was just one man, alone. He could not kill enough of the demons to make a real difference. He knew he was fighting a losing battle.

So he sent a message to the leaders of the demons, to the Five Lords of Pain. He told them that he would take on the five of them, one by one, in single combat. If he defeated them all, they would agree to leave the earth and take their demon armies with them. They would agree, also, never to harm another human.

The message was carried to the Five Lords by a certain demon called Yellow Nine-Tail. Yamada had said he would spare Yellow Nine-Tail's life only if he went crawling to his masters and told them about Yamada's challenge. The Five Lords were furious with Yellow Nine-Tail for letting himself be used as a messenger by a human. They tore him to pieces.

They were furious with Yoshiro Yamada too. How dare he! How dare a mere *man* challenge arch-demons to fight duels with them! Who did he think he was?

The Five Lords were so angry, and so proud, that they agreed to take up Yamada's challenge. He was only a human, after all. He couldn't beat *them*. They had the power of the Element Gems on their side. They would squash this upstart human like a fly!

The Five Lords of Pain met Yamada at the battle site, which was on the lower slopes of Mount Fuji in Japan. One after another, they took him on in single combat. One after another, the great samurai beat them.

Arch-demons could not be killed as lesser demons could. But Yamada struck each of the Five Lords through the heart with his sword, and cut out their Element Gems. Without the source of his power, each Lord of Pain was left weak and helpless, hardly alive.

Yoshiro Yamada took the Element Gems and hid them. Then he went back to the Five Lords and ordered them to keep their promise. He had beaten them. Now they must take their armies and go. They must find somewhere else to live, and leave the earth alone.

The Five Lords of Pain knew of another world. It was a place that was like this world but different. It was the earth's dark twin, linked to it as a shadow is linked to the object that casts it. It was a place of rocky landscapes and harsh weather, where the sun shone red and the seas burned like acid.

It was a place which might well be described as a living Hell.

The Five Lords of Pain limped off into this world, with their demon army.

They stayed in their world for 30 years, waiting for the time to be right and plotting against Yoshiro Yamada. It took them as long as that to recover their strength and get back their power, so they could order their Element Gems to return to them. They built themselves new bodies at the same time, making themselves even more powerful than they had been before.

Then the Lords of Pain returned to the earth, just the five of them. They wished to have their revenge on Yamada for foiling their plan. Their hatred of him was without bounds.

By then, Yoshiro Yamada was a very old man, at the end of his life. The Five Lords of Pain attacked him at his farm. Yamada fought back bravely, but time had left his body stiff and creaky. Age had slowed his sword arm. He could not win.

The Five Lords of Pain tore him limb from limb.

Yamada's adult son, Ren, was out working in the fields. When he heard his father's dying screams, he came running. He arrived at the farmhouse to find the Five Lords of Pain standing round the body of Yoshiro Yamada, with evil smiles on their faces.

Without thinking, Ren shouted at the Five Lords.

"You!" he cried, tears flowing down his cheeks. "Demons! Killers! I know who you are, and I am not afraid of you. 30 years ago you made a promise to my father. You said that if he won his duels with you, you would never harm another human being. But now you have. So hear this. I pray to all the gods. In their name, I curse you and all your kind. The earth will never be yours. If you try to take it by force, there will always be a Yamada to stop you. I, and my son, and his son, and his son's son, will stand against you, and so it shall be for all the ages to come. To take this world from us, you will have to fight a Yamada, as you fought my father 30 years ago. That is how it will happen for ever and ever. This curse shall bind all five of you, o Lord of the

Mountain, o Lord of the Typhoon, o Lord of Tears, o Lord of the Void, o Lord of Fire. Hear the words of Ren Yamada, son of Yoshiro Yamada, the man who defeated you in fair combat and whom you have now betrayed with your foul deed. Hear me and obey!"

The Five Lords of Pain scoffed at Ren. How could this human hope to bind them to a curse? His words were just words. They had no meaning. They were just an empty threat.

But the gods were listening. The gods heard Ren's prayer, and they agreed among themselves that what Ren had said must be so. The Five Lords of Pain had gone back on their promise to Yoshiro Yamada, and it was only fair that they pay for that. The universe must always be in balance. For every down there must be an up. For every wrong there must be a right.

Therefore the gods answered Ren's prayer and gave his curse power. Great power.

The Five Lords of Pain were sent screeching back to their world, the earth's shadow twin. And for the next 30 years they stayed there, till they were able once again to return to attack our world.

And during that time, Ren Yamada kept the Element Gems of the Five Lords. And he began training his son, Katsuo, in the martial arts, just as he himself had been trained by his father, Yoshiro. By the time Katsuo was grown up, he had become a master warrior, and was ready to meet the Five Lords of Pain in combat. And he beat them.

And so it went, 30 years at a time, on and on. The Yamada family was never without a first-born son and each one had the same task; he must defeat the Five Lords of Pain in combat.

So began the Contest.

Chapter 5

A Hero No One Had Ever Heard Of

Tom thought about the legend all the way home.

He knew that events in the legend had happened so long ago that nobody remembered anything about it any more. The demons had destroyed much of the world. It took ages for the human race to recover and rebuild afterwards, and get things back to normal. In time, people began to forget about the demons. They chose to do this, in fact. The demons were gone, sent away by the gods to their shadow world. It was better to act as if they had never existed. Life was easier that way.

People still told stories about the demons, usually beside a fire on dark nights. Scary tales to frighten the children. And frighten some of the grown-ups as well. But in the end everyone began to think that that was all the demons had ever been – just something out of a story. Fiction. You found them in books. You whispered about them. You drew pictures of them and maybe made models of them. You thought you saw them, but you never did. Some people believed they had talked to them. Some even thought they had made pacts with them. But it wasn't real, any of it. The demons had become nothing but an old, old memory.

Yoshiro Yamada's bravery had been forgotten too. No one knew anything about him now. Nor did anyone know about the Contest. It was a secret. It had to be, for everyone's peace of mind. People didn't need to know that every 30 years the fate of the planet hung in the balance, and that one person stood between the human race and a demon invasion. Life was scary enough anyway, most of all these days, with climate change and terrorists and nuclear weapons and everything else that was going on. There was so much fear in the world already. No one needed any more.

Yoshiro Yamada should have been remembered as the greatest hero ever. The same went for all the other Yamadas who had fought in Contests.

But there was no glory for them. No fame. They did what they did, and people would never hear about it and never thank them for it. For each of them, the only reward was knowing that the world was safe again for another 30 years.

Tom felt glum. He too was risking his life in the Contest now. Who would congratulate him if he won? His mother. Dragon. That was it. No one else. Even if he tried to reveal the truth about the Contest to the world, who would believe him? No one. Demons? Element Gems? Five duels to the death? People would laugh and mock. They would say it was just a story. They might even call him crazy.

A hero no one had ever heard of. That was the sad fate of every first-born son of the Yamada line. That was all Tom would ever be.

Tom turned the corner into his street and spotted someone sitting on the doorstep to his house. It was Sharif.

At first Tom was really pleased. He hadn't seen his friend for days.

Then he saw Sharif's face. Sharif looked totally fed up.

Tom knew why. He felt ashamed.

"Hey, Sharif!" he called out, putting on a broad smile. "How's it going?"

48

"Oh, so you *are* alive," said Sharif crossly. "I was beginning to wonder. I've sent you about a thousand texts. I've left messages on your voicemail. Not one word in reply from you. Would it kill you just to check your phone once in a while?"

"Yeah, look, sorry about that. I've been really busy."

"It's the school holidays," said Sharif, "remember? No lessons, no homework, none of that. How *can* you be busy?"

"Well, there's been this and that to do," Tom said. He knew how lame it sounded.

"What sort of this and that?"

"My music lessons, for starters." That was the cover story for Tom's training sessions with Dragon. He told everyone he was learning to play the violin.

"Oh, yes," said Sharif flatly. "Your music lessons. That takes care of two hours out of each day. How about the rest?"

"Er … um … it's kind of hard to explain," said Tom. In fact he was spending almost the whole of every day at the *dojo*. He needed all the training he could get, now that the Contest had started.

Sharif's face looked sly. "Is it a girl, Tom?"

"No."

"Come on, you can tell me. I bet it is. And I bet I know who, as well. It's Debbie Williams. I've seen her looking at you in class. Seen you looking at her too. You've always fancied her."

"Do not!" said Tom, but it was true, he did fancy Debbie Williams. Then again, just about every boy in Year 10 fancied Debbie Williams. Even though she wore glasses. Not many girls could make glasses sexy, but Debbie Williams could.

And Tom *had* noticed Debbie gazing at him across the classroom sometimes. Across the lunchroom too. She glanced away whenever his eyes met hers. But then she would always sneak another quick look at him, before carrying on talking to her girlfriends.

"I mean, she's fit and all," Tom went on, "but way too brainy for me. If we went out on a date, Debbie'd want to talk about books or French films or whatever, and I'd be going on about *World of Warcraft* and *Doctor Who* and stuff. It'd never work."

"But you don't know that for sure," Sharif said. "And you never will unless you ask her out."

"Well, maybe," said Tom. "But she might not want to go on a date with me in the first place."

"So if you aren't seeing a girl," said Sharif, "what's up?" He looked upset and hurt. "Are you trying to avoid me? Are we not friends any more and you haven't had the guts to tell me? Am I being given the brush-off here? Is that what it is?"

"No!" exclaimed Tom. "No, of course not, Sharif. God no, mate. Nothing like that."

"Phew."

"No, it's just … I really have been busy. And I really can't explain to you why."

"International man of mystery," said Sharif.

"I'd *like* to explain why," Tom said. "I just can't. It's not possible."

"I see."

"Does that make sense?"

"None at all," said Sharif. "Is it meant to?"

"Well, yeah. Sort of. Look, Sharif, what I can tell you is that I'm in the middle of something big. Something really big. We're talking humungous. And it's going to go on for quite a while." He added, "I hope."

"Quite a while?"

"Several months," said Tom. "Right into the autumn, if all goes well. And during that time I'm going to have a lot on my plate."

"A lot of what? Of this stuff you're not allowed to explain?"

"Yes. Yes, that's just it," said Tom. "It looks as if I'm even going to have to take some time off school, several weeks maybe. My mum's been dealing with the Head. Trying to fix it all. She's even hoping to get my GCSEs put back a year."

"That would suck," said Sharif.

"Yeah, I know," said Tom. "Thing is, mate, I'd love to be hanging out with you, mucking about on the computer, and listening to sounds and that. Honest I would. I just think that's going to be a bit … difficult for the time being."

"Difficult." Sharif's voice was frosty.

"We still can do that stuff. We will. But only now and then. Whenever I can fit it in."

"And that's how it's going to be? Till the autumn?"

"Yeah, till late autumn."

Sharif thought about this. "OK. So let me get this straight. I'll be your friend still, but only when it's handy for you."

"That's not what I'm saying," said Tom.

"No," said Sharif, "but it's what you mean."

"No, it isn't."

"Because – forgive me if I'm wrong – but that's not what being friends is all about, Tom," said Sharif. "Not in my book. Friends are there for each other all the time. Not just when it suits one of them."

"Sharif, trust me, this isn't what I want. This isn't about me at all. It isn't about you either. If it wasn't for this thing I'm involved with ..."

"The humungous something that you can't talk about."

"Yeah, that. If it wasn't for that, life would be simple. We'd be goofing around together like always. But ..."

Tom shrugged. There was nothing else he could say to defend himself. He couldn't tell Sharif about the Contest. That left a huge hole in his excuses that he had no way of filling.

He had to hope that Sharif would understand and forgive him.

But it seemed as if Sharif wasn't in the mood to forgive today.

"You know what, Tom?" he said. "I'm not stupid. This *is* a brush-off. I can tell. You don't want to be seen with your Asian pal any more. Well, fine."

"Hey, I'm half Asian," said Tom. "Don't play the racist card with me."

"Different sort of Asian," said Sharif. "You're the OK kind of Asian. I'm not. But you know what gets me?"

"What?"

"You can't even come up with a half-decent lie for not wanting to see me any more. You just jabber on about some big thing ..."

"Some big thing that's real," Tom pointed out, "and that I'm having to take time off school for."

"But it's rubbish, Tom," said Sharif. "It's just rubbish. You know it. So do I. And you're pathetic." He spat out the word. "Pathetic. You don't want me around any more? That's cool. Up yours."

Sharif spun on his heel and strode off down the street.

"Sharif!" Tom called out.

Sharif didn't stop walking.

"Sharif! Listen! Come back!"

Sharif held up a middle finger, still walking.

"Sharif," Tom said softly.

Sharif turned the corner at the far end of the street.

"Sharif," said Tom, "you stupid idiot."

But it wasn't Sharif's fault, Tom knew that.

It was his own fault.

No, that wasn't true.

It was the Contest's fault. The Contest was to blame.

The Contest had just cost Tom his best friend.

And he couldn't help asking himself how much more it would cost him before it was over.

Chapter 6
Time for a New TV

Tom was in his bedroom when it happened. He was at his laptop, working on an email to Sharif. He thought he might be able to explain himself better in writing, although he wasn't having much luck. He kept bumping up against the same problem: how to talk about the Contest without giving away anything about the Contest. It was like trying to describe an elephant without using the words "grey", "trunk" or "big ears". Or for that matter "elephant".

So Tom hadn't got much further than the subject heading for the email, which was "Sorry". And he was about to give up trying.

He wasn't sure if Sharif would read an email from him anyway. Most likely he wouldn't even open it. He'd take one look at the sender's address, and click on Delete.

Suddenly there was a loud noise from the living room. An ear-splitting *crackkk!*

Tom jumped in his seat. In the living room, his mother let out a startled yelp.

Tom went to see what was going on.

The TV had just blown up.

It was a large, old-fashioned kind of TV, a bulky silver box that took up most of one corner of the room. Its screen was now gone. All that was left was a black hole, with triangles of broken glass all round it, like teeth in a shark's mouth. More broken glass lay on the carpet in front of the TV.

Tom's mother was on the sofa, sitting clutching her knees to her chest. She looked white with alarm.

"Gave me the shock of my life!" she said. "I thought I was going to have a heart attack. One moment, the BBC news. The next – *boom*."

"What made it do that?" Tom asked. But he had a feeling he knew the answer.

He was right. Something took shape inside the jagged opening that had been the TV screen.

It was a parchment scroll.

Tom bent down and pulled it out carefully from inside the TV.

The scroll was tied with a black ribbon. He undid the ribbon, then passed the scroll to his mother.

"I expect it's a little note from the Lord of the Void," he said. "Challenging me to a duel."

61

Jane Yamada unrolled the scroll and peered at the *kanji* message on it. She nodded.

"'From the Lord of the Void,'" she read aloud, "'king of empty space, whose mercy is as cold as the deepest, darkest pit. To the son of the Yamada clan, who is truly nothing, less than nothing.'"

"Yeah, yeah, I know," said Tom, as though talking to the Lord of the Void himself. "You're fantastic, I'm not, blah blah blah. Get on with it, Voidy."

"'We shall meet at sunset, two days from now,'" his mother went on. "'The site of the duel shall be that place that is known as Ayers Rock and also as Uluru.'"

"What!?" Tom yelled. "Australia?"

His mother quickly read the last few Japanese symbols on the scroll. "Then there's a whole lot of stuff about how he's going to win and you aren't," she said. "Much like last time, with the Lord of the Mountain."

"Don't tell me. He's going to suck the life out of me, right?"

"More or less. How did you know?"

"They like their themes, the Lords of Pain," Tom said. "The Lord of the Mountain was all about rocks and dirt. The Lord of the Void seems to be all about space and emptiness." He shrugged. "I took a wild guess."

He frowned.

"But Australia, Mum," he said. "*Australia.* That's the other side of the world. And we have to be there the day after tomorrow?"

"Then we'd best get cracking," said his mother, standing up. "I'll get onto the internet and make some bookings. You phone Dragon and tell him we've had our orders for the next duel. Oh, and then you can sweep up those bits of glass."

"Is that really my job?" said Tom.

"It is now," snapped his mother. She hurried off to her study, all business-like and full of energy.

"Mum?" Tom said.

She stopped. "Yes?"

"You're being very calm about this all of a sudden."

"Am I?"

"Yeah. Up till now you've been a wreck. Then all of a sudden you're, like, Mrs Super Cool and In Charge."

His mother thought for a moment. "Well," she said, "now I have something real to do. I'm not just sitting on my bum waiting. Besides, every minute counts. If we don't reach the site of the duel in time ..."

She made a grim face. She didn't need to finish the sentence.

"Fair point," said Tom. He glanced at the remains of the TV. "And there is a bright side to this."

"There is?"

"The telly's trashed. So now we can buy that 40-inch flat-screen I've been bugging you about."

Jane Yamada almost laughed.

Almost.

Chapter 7
Jimmy Blue

They were all worn out by the journey.

Tom's mother had bought business-class tickets for herself, Tom and Dragon. So they had large, plush seats on the plane, great food, fine wine, and even a free neck massage.

"Good to be a bit spoiled," Jane Yamada said as the plane took off. "I can afford it. We deserve it."

"The good life is the enemy of happiness, Mrs Yamada," said Dragon with a sweet smile. "But not always."

"And," Tom's mother said to Tom, "this way you should arrive calm and relaxed for your ... you-know-what." She didn't want to say the word "Contest" in public.

But Tom couldn't relax. He tried to sleep, but the flight was bumpy, and his nerves were starting to get the better of him. He watched endless movies on the screen of his personal TV, which came out of the arm-rest of his seat. When he got off the plane at Sydney Airport 24 hours later, his eyes were red and his head felt wobbly like a balloon.

There was a hold-up at the airport. After Dragon's luggage had been through the x-ray machine, the men in charge opened it all up. They found a set of very nasty-looking weapons inside one of his bags. The problem was soon sorted out, however. Dragon produced the permits which allowed him to take the weapons abroad with him.

"It's for a martial arts competition," he told the customs officers. Which was sort of true.

Tom, his mother and Dragon then got on a smaller jet, which flew them out to a town that lay right at the very heart of Australia. It took an hour and a half to get there. Australia, Tom saw, was a truly huge country.

The town's name was Alice Springs. At the airport there, they were met by a man called Jimmy Blue. He was the driver who was going to take them to Uluru. Jimmy was an Aborigine. Aborigines had lived in Australia for thousands of years before the white men came. He had a chubby face, a broad smile, and eyes the colour of dark chocolate.

"First time in Oz, mate?" he asked Tom as he carried their bags to the car. The car was a huge, long black limo.

Tom nodded.

"Like it?"

"It's hot," Tom said, fanning his face with his hand. Being outdoors was like being blasted by a great big hair-dryer.

"Nah, this ain't hot," said Jimmy. "You should've been here in January. It was a hundred degrees in the shade then. This is the cool season, and a few weeks from now it can get pretty chilly. You've come at just the right time. Hit the bulls-eye, you might say."

Luckily, the inside of the limo was like a fridge. Jimmy had turned the air-conditioning up full.

They drove out from Alice Springs into the Outback, the vast empty desert that took up most of the centre of the country. The road ran in a straight line, with nothing to see on either side but red sand and plants that looked brittle and burnt. Tom stared out of the window, wishing he could just nod off to sleep. At one point he spotted the body of an animal next to the road. It must have been hit by a car, a couple of days ago. Its belly was huge and swollen, and flies were buzzing all over it. Tom saw its powerful hind legs and its long tail and knew that it was a kangaroo. He thought to himself, *Great. My first sight of a kangaroo in the wild, and it's dead.* He was already feeling low and now his mood sank even lower.

Four hours and 450 kilometres later, they reached Uluru.

"There it is," said Jimmy Blue. "Uluru. That's what my people call it. It's a holy place to us Aborigines. I guess you must know that already. The souls of our dead live there. We believe the rock was formed when the world was first made. We tell a story about two giant boys playing in the mud after a rainfall. They built Uluru out of the mud. Of course, everyone knows the rock is just a big hunk of sandstone sticking up out of the ground, part of a mountain range that got worn away by the wind and rain over millions of years. But I like the story about the two giant boys better."

Tom peered ahead. Uluru, to him, looked like an island rising steeply out of the sea – only a sea of sand, not of water. The sides of the rock were carved into gullies. It was bright orange and seemed almost to glow against the pure blue sky.

"Do you know, there was snow on top of the rock yesterday," said Jimmy. "It melted pretty fast, but still. Snow, in the middle of the Outback. Got all of the TV weather men in a tizzy, that did. They called it a freak event. Talked about an area of sudden low pressure. Said it had never happened before and was not likely to happen ever again." He chuckled. "Ah, but what do they know? Them white fellas with their satellite maps and their rain gauges and what-have-you. What do *they* know about the weather?" He clucked his tongue.

"It *has* happened before, Jimmy?" Tom asked.

"Sure, mate! Not for a while. Not in the memory of anyone alive right now. But my people, we go back a long way and we remember things. We tell stories from hundreds of years ago, even thousands of years. It's snowed on Uluru before. And that's not all. There have been weird fogs. Thunder clouds that rain just on the rock and nowhere else. The place draws strange weather to it. That's one of the reasons we respect it and worship it. Uluru's got some real power, mate. It's not just some big, beautiful lump of stone in the middle of nowhere."

No, thought Tom. *There have been duels here. That's what the strange weather is there for. To hide the duels from the eyes of the world.*

Jimmy found a space for the limo in a large car park not far from the rock.

"Want me to give you a guided tour?" he asked. "I know my way round the place pretty well."

"No, thank you, Mr Blue," said Tom's mother. "We can manage on our own."

"Sure. No worries," said Jimmy. "I'll just wait here, then."

Dragon got the bag with the weapons in it out of the boot of the car. He started walking towards Uluru. Tom's mother followed him. Tom was about to go too, when Jimmy stopped him.

"Just one thing, mate," he said.

"Yes?"

Jimmy's dark chocolate eyes were serious. "Good luck."

"Wha–?"

"Yeah, yeah," said Jimmy with a wave of his hand. "I'm not supposed to know who you are or what you're here to do. But I do. Like I said, my people remember things. We pass stories on to one another. You've been here before. I don't mean you yourself. I mean your kind. Members of your family came here long ago. And we know why."

"I really have no idea what you're talking about," Tom said.

"Fair go. It's all a secret. I get it." Jimmy winked. "I'm just saying, do your best. Give that bad fella one for me. OK?"

Tom tried to keep a straight face, but couldn't.

"OK," he said, with a half smile. "I will."

"Good on you," said Jimmy Blue.

"Tom!" called Dragon.

"Coming!" Tom called back, and set off after him.

Jimmy's words had given him a boost. All at once Tom didn't feel nearly so tired.

He wasn't going to be a hero no one had ever heard of after all.

Someone understood what he was doing and why. Someone cared.

Thank you, Jimmy Blue.

Chapter 8
Hail Storm

They sat down among some tall, spindly trees near the base of Ayers Rock. Dragon looked at his watch. It was late afternoon. The sun was due to set in an hour or so.

"Time to get ready," he said.

Tom put on his white combat *gi*. After some thought, Dragon armed him with a *katana* sword and the *chigiriki*.

"The Lord of the Void always uses some kind of sword," Dragon said. "It's best to match one sword against another. But he's in the habit of wearing armour too, and the *chigiriki* can be effective against that."

"Anything else I need to know about him?" Tom asked.

"His element is the void," said Dragon. "He will have some special skill linked to empty space."

"That's it? You don't know what this skill is?"

Dragon gave a sigh of regret. "It changes from Contest to Contest. Remember, we talked about this? The Five Lords make up new duel bodies for themselves each time. They equip themselves in different ways, depending on how the mood takes them. There's no telling what the Lord of the Void will have come up with for this duel. You just have to watch and learn and be flexible. That's all there is to it."

"God, I wish there were cheats and hints for the Contest," Tom said. "You know, stuff you could look up on the internet or get from a magazine. Even just a teach-yourself manual would be nice."

"Life isn't a computer game," said Tom's mother.

"I do know that," Tom said. "It's just – sometimes it would be easier if it was."

The sky was getting very dark. All of a sudden the bright sunlight was gone. Black clouds had come up above Uluru, like an immense ink stain on the sky.

Within minutes, the air had turned cold and damp.

Then, without warning, hail began to fall.

It came down in clumps, some of them as big as golf balls. It hammered the ground. Soon the sand was covered with blobs of white ice, and still the hail kept falling. People ran for their cars and tour buses, covering their heads and yelling. Tom, his mother and

Dragon stayed put. The trees just about saved them from the hail storm.

The hail moved away from Uluru, towards the car park. It was like a curtain, keeping the tourists at bay. The black clouds were still hanging above the rock.

Dragon got to his feet. Tom took that as a signal to do the same.

"Tom ..." said his mother.

Jane Yamada wasn't good with goodbyes. She wasn't good with I-love-yous either.

She hugged her son quickly.

Tom and Dragon crunched off across the carpet of hailstones, towards Uluru.

Chapter 9
The Lord of the Void

Tom and Dragon climbed the rock along the path used by tourists. There was a chain railing beside the path which they could hold onto and use to help pull themselves up. The journey was only half a mile, but it was hard work because the side of the rock was so steep. The hailstones didn't help. Tom and Dragon kept slipping and sliding on them.

Halfway up, they stopped to rest.

"I'm a Contest fighter, get me out of here," Tom joked.

Dragon looked blank. Tom thought it likely Dragon didn't watch a lot of TV. Most likely he didn't even *have* a TV.

They started to climb again.

The sun was shining when they got near the top. It was low in the sky and glowed red above the horizon, beyond the edge of the mass of black cloud.

Dragon had stopped now, knowing he was not allowed to go any further. What Tom had to do next, he had to do on his own.

Dragon waved, telling Tom to carry on up the path.

"Don't forget to bring back that Element Gem," he said.

Tom covered the last few metres up onto the summit of Uluru. A strong wind whipped around his legs. The view was amazing. He could see so far in every direction, it was as if he was looking out over the whole of Australia, all the way to the sea.

Ahead of him an oval shape shone just above the rock. It was the size of a doorway. It was white, like mist, and shimmered with rainbow patterns.

The barrier. The gateway to the arena, the site of the duel.

Tom took a few more steps. He felt light as a feather as he passed through the white oval. He knew this feeling from his last duel, at Stonehenge.

The feeling faded. Now Tom was in another place. He was still standing on top of a vast rock in the middle of a plain, like Uluru. The carpet of hail-stones had vanished, and the landscape around the rock looked different. The desert sand was a deeper red, almost the colour of blood, and there were craters in it. Tom could have been on Mars, perhaps, or the moon. In fact, Tom was looking at part of the demons' world.

Then Tom saw faces peeking out at him from behind ridges nearby. He heard the sound of high-pitched laughter.

Demons.

They were watching him, like last time. They were here to witness the fight. They'd come to see the Lord of the Void do battle with Tom and, they hoped, kill him. Then, if Tom was dead, the way would be clear for the demons to come through onto the earth and take it over, with the Five Lords of Pain leading the way.

Tom drew his *katana* from its sheath. He didn't feel tired any more. Not a bit of it. His senses felt sharp. He was alert and clear-headed.

"Lord of the Void!" he shouted out. "I'm ready. Where are you? Show yourself!"

Nothing happened.

Then the air in front of Tom seemed to suck in on itself. It swirled round and round, like water going down a plughole. Then it snapped back to normal with a loud *shwoop*. At the same time a figure appeared, out of nowhere.

The Lord of the Void.

He was taller than Tom, but only by a little. He was covered from head to toe in shiny black armour. The armour gleamed like the shell of a beetle.

The watching demons howled with glee.

"A-ha," said the Lord of the Void to Tom. His voice echoed inside the armour, like a man speaking in a cave. "There you are. The boy who reckons he's a fully grown champion."

There was a slit in the face-plate of the helmet he was wearing. Two bright red eyes peered out through this, gazing at Tom.

"I was worried, you know," he said. "It became clear that I would have to get back my Element Gem and make myself a new duel body early this time. I was not sure if I could do this. I knew I could get myself back to full strength, even if it was 15 years too soon. But still I was worried about facing you all the same."

The Lord of the Void gave a booming laugh.

"And now I see how foolish I was!" he said. "My fears faded away the moment I laid eyes on you. Look how small and weedy you are. This is going to be easy."

Tom would have liked to think the Lord of the Void was talking rubbish. But he had to agree, he was still a boy. He wondered where the arch-demon's weapon was. Dragon had told him the Lord of the Void carried a sword, but there was no sword as far as Tom could see. All the arch-demon had was his bare hands and his armour.

"Get ready to die, Yamada," the Lord of the Void growled.

"Get ready to lose," Tom said in reply, and attacked.

Chapter 10
Shwoop

Tom jumped high into the air, swinging his *katana* in a perfect arc.

He had seen a gap in the Lord of the Void's armour. It was between the helmet and the neck guard.

The sword blow would cut the Lord of the Void's head clean off. That was how Tom had killed the Lord of the Mountain. He was sure the same trick would work here.

There was a *shwoop*. The *katana* swished through empty air.

Tom hit the ground. He spun round on his toes.

Where had the Lord of the Void gone? He'd been there a moment ago. Then he'd vanished.

Shwoop.

The sound came from behind Tom. Tom spun round.

The Lord of the Void was standing there. He lifted one fist. He threw a punch at Tom.

Tom ducked in the nick of time. The punch missed, whooshing above his head. Just as well, too. The Lord of the Void was wearing a metal glove. Tom would have been knocked out cold if the punch had hit him.

Still bent down, Tom lashed out with his *katana*, aiming at the Lord of the Void's knee. There was another gap in his armour there.

Again a *shwoop*. The air twisted and spun, and the Lord of the Void was gone.

So that was his special power. He could jump from place to place in the blink of an eye. He could teleport.

Tom got up and looked around.

The Lord of the Void *shwooped* back into view, a few metres away.

"Now that must annoy you," the arch-demon cackled to Tom. "You can't lay a finger on me!"

"Yeah, well, you're not exactly spot-on with your punches either, are you?" Tom yelled back at him.

The Lord of the Void shrugged. "You're fast, I'll give you that, Yamada. But I'll get you all the same."

Shwoop.

He vanished, then was back a moment later, standing right in front of Tom. He threw himself at Tom with both arms stretched out in front of him. Tom jumped sideways and stuck his foot out. The Lord of the Void tripped over Tom's foot and fell. He landed flat on the hard rock beneath him with a ringing *clang*.

Tom stood over him, his sword held high.

Once again, the Lord of the Void *shwooped* out of sight. He *shwooped* back a safe distance away.

"This is getting boring," Tom said. "Why don't you stand still for a moment? All these demons want to see a proper fight. Not watch you dancing about like a big old fairy."

Some of the demons giggled at Tom's remark.

"What did you say?" snarled the Lord of the Void.

"You heard. I told you you're dancing about like a big old fairy."

The Lord of the Void let out a roar of anger. "No one insults me like that!"

"Really? I just did," Tom said smartly. He was hoping the Lord of the Void would lose his temper. Then he might get careless.

And he did.

He *shwooped* himself into a position directly behind Tom. He grabbed Tom's arms with both hands.

"There!" he cried. "Now I have you, and I'm going to rip your arms off. Is that what you wanted?"

"Kind of," said Tom. He flipped his sword round so that the tip was aiming backwards. Then he thrust it at the Lord of the Void's middle. It slid between the chest-plate of the armour and the waist section below. Tom felt the *katana* bite into soft flesh. He rammed it deep, and heard the Lord of the Void howl in pain.

Shwoop.

The Lord of the Void was gone yet again. Tom spun round, looking in all directions. No sign of the arch-demon.

No sign of Tom's *katana* either. It had been sticking into the Lord of the Void when he teleported. The moment he was gone, the sword was gone too.

Tom plucked the *chigiriki* from his belt. Good thing he had a back-up weapon.

Time passed. It was clear that the watching demons were puzzled. They were chatting and shaking their heads. Tom could guess what they were saying to one another. Where was the Lord of the Void? Had he run away? Was he hiding from the Yamada boy? The boy had hurt him. Was he too scared to face him now?

Tom was thinking that this could mean he had won the duel. Had it been that easy? He didn't think so, somehow.

At last – *shwoop*.

The Lord of the Void was back.

Then he was gone.

Then he was back again.

He seemed to be having trouble with his teleporting. He flickered into and out of sight several times. He came and went like a light bulb with a loose connection, fizzling on, then off.

At last there was one last almighty *SHWOOP*. The air stretched and shrank, then snapped back on itself. The Lord of the Void was left kneeling on the ground. Tom's sword was still sticking out from his belly.

"Curse you, Yamada!" he said. "The pain ... I can't think properly. I can't focus my mind."

"Oh, dear, poor you," said Tom, as if he was really sorry. "You can't teleport any more? What a pity. Now you'll just have to stand there and fight like a man."

He started to swing the *chigiriki*.

The Lord of the Void rose to his feet slowly. He was stiff. He grasped the hilt of the *katana*. He tried to pull the sword out of him but it was stuck fast. He pulled and tugged at it, hissing with pain and effort. In the end, however, all he did was snap off the blade.

With a snort of disgust, he tossed away the broken-off hilt.

"You haven't even got a weapon," Tom crowed. "I think you'd better just let me finish this off quickly. I can't bear to see you suffer."

"No weapon?" replied the Lord of the Void. He began to laugh. "Well, if you say so, Yamada. Come and get me, then."

Dragon's words flashed through Tom's mind: *Never think your enemy is unarmed, just because he does not seem to have a weapon.*

Tom decided not to follow this advice, however. Dragon had told him that the Lord of the Void used a sword of some sort, but he was clearly not carrying one now, or any other kind of weapon. His main form of attack was the teleporting, and he could no longer do that. Which left him with nothing but his armour. And Tom had already shown that the armour wasn't a perfect form of defence.

Tom brought the *chigiriki* up above his head. Then he ran at the Lord of the Void.

He couldn't believe what happened next.

Chapter 11
Black Swords

The Lord of the Void snatched off the section of armour that covered the top of his right leg. The piece of metal began to melt and change as soon as he touched it. It flowed like hot candle wax. Then suddenly it was solid once more. It had re-formed itself into a narrow, pointed shape.

A sword. A broad, black, gleaming sword.

All this took place in less than a second. The Lord of the Void had somehow created a sword for himself in the time it took Tom to reach him.

Tom couldn't stop. He had built up too much speed. He had no choice but to swing the *chigiriki* at the Lord of the Void, as he'd planned to do in the first place. The spiked weight on the end of the chain struck the arch-demon's armour with a *clunk*. At the same time, the Lord of the Void slashed at Tom with the black metal sword. Tom jumped aside in order to avoid the blow.

But he was too slow.

Just a fraction of an instant too slow.

"Aargh!"

The sword's blade sliced into Tom's left arm, just above the elbow.

The sword cut hard. It cut deep.

At first Tom felt nothing but a horrible coldness.

Then, all at once, there was heat – a fierce burning heat.

After that came pain, terrible pain hitting him with stunning force, like a train.

He staggered away from the Lord of the Void. He couldn't move his left arm. It hung by his side, useless. Blood gushed from the wound, pouring over his forearm, then his hand. It fell in trickling drips from his fingers.

The Lord of the Void laughed a hollow, mocking laugh.

"You didn't see that coming, did you, Yamada?"

Tom clenched his teeth. The pain from his arm seemed to fill his entire body, like a flood of boiling hot water. His head was reeling. He thought he was about to pass out. Everything was a blur. The world seemed far away from him. The ground beneath his feet wobbled. The solid rock of Uluru seemed to have turned to jelly.

Get a grip, he told himself. *Ignore the pain. You must not faint now.*

Dragon had taught him that you could control pain. It could be overcome, however bad it was.

"You must rise above it," Dragon liked to say. "Become an eagle in your thoughts, and fly up away from the pain, as an eagle flies high above the mountains."

Pain was all in the mind. It was a distress signal from your body which your mind could block out. If you tried hard enough. If you had the willpower.

Just then Tom saw the Lord of the Void coming at him. That black sword was high in the air. The Lord of the Void was laughing to himself.

An eagle, Tom thought. *Flying high.*

He had an image of himself in the blue sky, hovering on wings. The sharp peaks of mountains lay far below, lost in cloud.

The pain faded. Tom's head cleared.

Not a moment too soon.

The Lord of the Void swung his sword at Tom's head. Tom's response was to swing out with his *chigiriki* and wrap its chain around the sword blade. He pulled. The sword flew from the Lord of the Void's hand. Tom cracked the *chigiriki* like a whip, and the sword came loose from the chain. It fell to the ground with a clatter several metres away.

The Lord of the Void stood still and simply took hold of another section of his armour. This time it was the piece that covered his left forearm.

Metal rippled and flowed, and now he had a fresh sword.

"And there's plenty more where that came from," the Lord of the Void added.

"Big fat deal," said Tom. In fact he didn't so much *say* this as *pant* it out. "More swords. Less armour."

And he cracked the *chigiriki* like a whip, aiming it at the Lord of the Void's right leg.

This was the leg that had been covered by the piece of armour that had become the Lord of the Void's first sword. It wasn't covered any more. The flesh had been laid bare.

The spikes on the weight dug into the thigh.

The Lord of the Void screamed.

Tom gave a tug on the *chigiriki*. It came free of the Lord of the Void's thigh, taking a chunk of flesh with it.

The arch-demon screamed again.

And while he was screaming, Tom used the *chigiriki* to yank the second sword from his grasp.

In a flash, the Lord of the Void changed yet another section of his armour into a sword.

But Tom clubbed the Lord of the Void's bare forearm with the chigiriki.

More flesh tore. There was more screaming.

Tom darted around the arch-demon, striking at spots where his body was not protected by his armour any more. The Lord of the Void lashed out wildly. He yelled with rage and pain.

Tom kept taking away swords with the *chigiriki*. The Lord of the Void kept making new ones, and as he did so kept leaving more of his body without armour. He grew madder and madder. He no longer seemed to care about defending himself. All he wanted was to hit Tom with a sword. But Tom would not stay still and would not be hit.

In the end the Lord of the Void had almost no armour left. Even his helmet was gone. His body was a mass of cuts and scrapes. His blood spattered the rocky ground around him. His used swords lay everywhere.

Tom hit him several more times with the *chigiriki*, and the Lord of the Void sank to his knees.

Tom stood in front of him, panting hard.

The Lord of the Void's red eyes glared at Tom. His face was white and weary, and very ugly too. His mouth was like a wasp's, made of several moving parts that were linked with one another. His nose was as flat as a pig's snout.

"You have won," he said. "But the Contest is far from over. Next you face the Lord of Tears. Compared with him, I am nothing. His power is great. He delights in causing suffering. To him the crying of children is a soft lullaby. It is music to his ears when women weep. To him – ”

“Oh, just shut *up*,” said Tom.

He hit the Lord of the Void on the head with the *chigiriki*, putting all the strength he had into the blow.

The Lord of the Void fell flat on his face. He twitched for a while. His throat gave a rattle. Then he lay still.

Tom looked down at the gash in his arm. The wound was long and deep. He saw something smooth and white inside the wound.

Bone. His own bone.

His head spun. He knew he was close to fainting. He had to get out of here.

Before he could return to his own world, however, there was something else he must do.

Tom picked up one of the many black swords that lay about. He bent over the Lord of the Void and placed the tip of the sword on the arch-demon's naked chest. He thrust down with the sword, one-handed. Then he began working the blade from side to side in a sawing action.

Soon he was done. He had cut a large hole in the Lord of the Void's ribcage. Tom reached down into the hole. He searched around like someone playing the Lucky Dip at a fair. His hand sloshed and glooped among the hot, sticky organs.

At last he found his prize and pulled it free.

The black Element Gem.

Tom got up. He dragged himself towards the white oval with the gem in his hand. He dived through the gateway to the other side.

Back in his own world he slumped to the ground. He lay flat out on the hail-stones that covered the rock. The cold and wet of the hail-stones seeped through his clothes, soaking his skin. He tried to get up but he had no more energy left. He simply could not move.

Everything went dark.

Chapter 12
The Black Element Gem

Dragon climbed to the top of Uluru. It was nearly night time. The duel must surely be over by now.

He found Tom lying on the ground.

"Tom …" Dragon said with a cluck of his tongue. "Look at you. Look at what you let the Lord of the Void do to you."

Dragon tore a strip of cloth from his own shirt. He wrapped it tight around Tom's arm to make a bandage. Tom needed to be taken to a hospital.

Dragon saw the black Element Gem lying in Tom's hand. He plucked it free from Tom's fingers. He held the gem up, studying it for a while in the last of the daylight.

The gem wasn't glowing now. It was like a ball of pure, solid black glass. Dragon could still sense the power deep inside the gem, but it was weak, like a faintly flickering flame, a spark in the night.

Dragon slipped it into his pocket. Then he picked up Tom, slung him over his back, and set off down the path that led to the base of the rock.

Chapter 13
Sharif

Sharif pressed the buzzer a third time.

He was standing on the front doorstep of Tom's house. It was morning, a little after seven o'clock. On the other side of the world, Dragon was carrying Tom down Uluru, although Sharif had no way of knowing this.

All Sharif could think was, where the hell *was* Tom? It was breakfast time. Tom would be home, surely. So would Mrs Yamada. She never left for work before 7.30.

But here was Sharif, pressing the buzzer button for Flat 3, and there was no reply. No voice on the intercom going, "Who is it?" Nothing.

Bloody hell! thought Sharif.

He'd come over to speak to Tom. To give Tom one last chance. He didn't want to lose Tom as a friend. He hated the idea of the two of them falling out. He hoped he could make Tom come clean, make him tell the truth, to explain what was going on in his life that was so important it left no room for his best mate. Maybe it was something Sharif could help him with. Wasn't there a saying? Something about a problem shared being a problem halved?

Sharif pressed the buzzer one last time, leaning on the button for nearly half a minute.

No answer.

That was that, then. Either Tom wasn't home, or he *was* home but he was refusing to see visitors. Perhaps he had looked out of a window and spotted Sharif coming up the street. Perhaps he was ignoring the buzzer on purpose.

I'm being paranoid, Sharif thought.

But was he?

Sharif turned away from the door, shoulders slumped. He walked slowly off down the street. He was going home – a ten-minute walk.

He didn't notice a figure gazing down at him from the roof of Tom's house.

Nor did he see this same figure start to move, crawling across the roof, leaping to the roof of the next house, and of the house after that.

It was a figure of a man dressed in white from head to toe, and it made no sound as it moved across the rooftops. It was as stealthy and silent as a cat, or a ghost.

111

It followed Sharif home.

It stalked him all the way to his front door.

Then it pounced.

List of Japanese Words

Ashiko: set of metal spikes that can be fixed to the bottom of the shoe. Used by ninjas for climbing and walking on ice, and also for self-defence

Chigiriki: type of club with a spiked, cylinder-shaped weight attached to a chain at one end

Dojo: a school which trains in the arts of one-to-one combat (martial arts)

Gi *(say it with a hard g, as in 'go')*: martial arts uniform. Loose trousers and a jacket tied at the waist with a cloth belt

Kanji: Japanese writing

Katana: long sword used by warriors, such as the the samurai (see picture on right)

Katsuo: male name; it means "victorious child"

Naginata: pole weapon ending in a long, curved blade

Sensei *(sen-say)*: polite name for a master or teacher

Ren: male name; it means "water lily"

Shuko: gloves with hooks on, used by ninjas for climbing; also known as cat claws

Tanto: 30-centimetre-long dagger

Yoshiro: male name; it means "lucky person"

Check out Tom's next duel in ...

The Lord of Tears

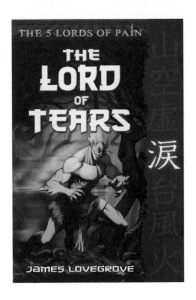

Tom faces the Lord of Tears.
As fast as lightning and twice as deadly.

Turn the page to read the start of the next book!

A Park in Tokyo

It was getting late. The sun was going down behind the sky-scrapers of Tokyo. The shadows were growing long in the district of Harajuku, where Tom was waiting.

Tom looked around, trying to spot the figure dressed in white. He'd seen it the night before. If the figure was what he thought it was, he was sure it would be back tonight.

Tom had been in Tokyo for two weeks. He'd spent the time hanging around in public areas of the city, places where he would get noticed. He was not trying to hide the fact that he was there. Indeed he'd been trying to stand out, trying to be obvious. He wanted to be spotted. He wanted to be found.

Then yesterday evening, in the Harajuku district, it had happened. He'd caught sight of a white figure watching him from some way off.

Harajuku was where lots of the local kids got together, dressed up as people from the worlds of manga, movies and music. They liked to walk around, looking at each other's costumes. Tom had seen super-heroes such as Spider-Man and Superman. He'd also seen girls dressed as Sailor Moon and boys dressed like the death god Ryuk from *Death Note*. There'd been robots, rock stars, and any number of street dancers and performers. It was crazy, like a cross between a meeting of sci-fi fans and a talent show.

At first the white figure had just seemed to Tom like just another kid in a costume, one who happened to be dressed like a ninja.

That was why no one else paid much notice to the white figure. But the white figure kept staring at Tom ... and he looked just how Tom had been told a Shinobi Ghost would look. His head was wrapped in a long scarf which acted as both hood and mask. His whole face was covered except for the eyes. And his eyes were pale and empty. White.

Like the eyes of a dead man.

Barrington Stoke would like to thank all its readers for commenting on the manuscript before publication and in particular:

Lizzie Alder
Richard Brant
Polly Byrne
Josh Caddy
Mary Campbell
Sean Campbell
John Cowe
Ryan Crowle
Alfie Duke
George Evans
Jake Francis
Robert Garside
Susan Gillespie
CJ Lethbridge
Tré Pusey
Sam Quarterman
Caroline Rowse
Rachael Sargent
Haydn Smallwood
Martisha Thompson
Jordan Truscott

Become a Consultant!

Would you like to be a consultant? Ask your parent, carer or teacher to contact us at the email address below – we'd love to hear from them! They can also find out more by visiting our website.

schools@barringtonstoke.co.uk
www.barringtonstoke.co.uk